I'm Going To READ!

These levels are meant only as guides;
you and your child can best choose a book that's right.

Level 1: Kindergarten – Grade 1 . . . Ages 4–6
- word bank to highlight new words
- consistent placement of text to promote readability
- easy words and phrases
- simple sentences built to make simple stories
- art and design help new readers decode text

Level 2: Grade 1 . . . Ages 6–7
- word bank to highlight new words
- rhyming texts introduced
- more difficult words, but vocabulary is still limited
- longer sentences and longer stories
- designed for easy readability

Level 3: Grade 2 . . . Ages 7–8
- richer vocabulary of up to 200 different words
- varied sentence structure
- high-interest stories with longer plots
- designed to promote independent reading

Level 4: Grades 3 and up . . . Ages 8 and up
- richer vocabulary of more than 300 different words
- short chapters, multiple stories, or poems
- more complex plots for the newly independent reader
- emphasis on reading for meaning

LEVEL 2

2 4 6 8 10 9 7 5 3 1

Published by Sterling Publishing Co., Inc.
387 Park Avenue South, New York, NY 10016
Text © 2006 by Harriet Ziefert Inc.
Illustrations © 2006 by Yukiko Kido
Distributed in Canada by Sterling Publishing
c/o Canadian Manda Group, 165 Dufferin Street,
Toronto, Ontario, Canada M6K 3H6
Distributed in the United Kingdom by GMC Distribution Services,
Castle Place, 166 High Street, Lewes, East Sussex, England BN7 1XU
Distributed in Australia by Capricorn Link (Australia) Pty. Ltd.
P.O. Box 704, Windsor, NSW 2756, Australia

I'm Going To Read is a trademark of Sterling Publishing Co., Inc.

Library of Congress Cataloging-in-Publication Data

Ziefert, Harriet.
  Fun Land fun! / Harriet Ziefert ; pictures by Yukiko Kido.
    p. cm.—(I'm going to read)
  Summary: Three friends spend an enjoyable day at the
  amusement park, riding roller coasters, driving bumper cars,
  and eating cotton candy.
  ISBN-13: 978-1-4027-3416-8
  ISBN-10: 1-4027-3416-6
  [1. Amusement parks—Fiction.] I. Kido, Yukiko, ill. II. Title. III. Series.

PZ7.Z487Ft 2006
[E]—dc22   2005034143

Sterling ISBN-13: 978-1-4027-3416-8
ISBN-10: 1-4027-3416-6

For information about custom editions, special sales, premium and
corporate purchases, please contact Sterling Special Sales
Department at 800-805-5489 or specialsales@sterlingpub.com.

FUN LAND FUN!

Pictures by Yukiko Kido

Sterling Publishing Co., Inc.
New York

FUN

Nomi went to Fun Land
with her friends.

Nomi and Kira rode
the Ferris wheel.
"I'm not scared,"
said Nomi. "Are you?"

Ken and Kira rode
the bumper cars.

bumper

"Watch out!"
yelled Nomi.

They all rode
on the roller coaster.
"I'm not scared,"
yelled Nomi.

Then they
went into the
fun house.

Kira was last.
Ken was next.

was into

FUN HOUSE

Nomi went first.

They heard funny noises.
Kira was a little scared.

But not Nomi!

They looked
at themselves.

"I'm fat!"
said Ken.

"I'm skinny!"
said Nomi.

They left the fun house
on a rolling insect!

snack   there's   bar

"I'm hungry!" said Nomi.
"Me too!" said Kira.

Ken pointed.
"There's a snack bar."

Nomi
got popcorn.

Kira got
cotton candy.

Ken had
peanuts.

asked

Ken asked, "Do you want to ride
on the roller coaster one more time?"

"I'll watch," said Nomi.
"I don't want to throw up."

"I'll ride with you,"
said Kira.

Ken looked a little green
when he came off the
roller coaster.

Kira was even greener!

And Nomi?
Her cheeks were
pretty pink!